Davy

Manni

Lina

Brigitte Weninger was born in Kufstein, Austria, and spent twenty years working as a kindergarten teacher before trying her hand at writing. She has since published more than fifty books, which have been translated into thirty languages worldwide. She continues to be heavily involved in promoting literacy and storytelling.

Eve Tharlet was born in France but spent much of her childhood in Germany. After graduating from the Superior School of Decorative Arts in Strasbourg, France, she began working as a freelance illustrator in 1981 and quickly received international acclaim. Her big breakthrough came with the series about Davy, the cute and cheeky bunny, which propelled her name around the world.

Copyright © 1996 by NordSüd Verlag AG, CH-8005, Zürich, Switzerland.
First published in Switzerland under the title *Ein Geschwisterchen für Pauli*.
English translation copyright © 1996 by NorthSouth Books, Inc., New York 10016.
Translated by Rosemary Lanning

First published under the title *Will You Mind the Baby, Davy?* in the United States, Great Britain, Canada, Australia, and New Zealand in 1996 by NorthSouth Books, Inc., an imprint of NordSüd Verlag AG, CH-8005 Zürich, Switzerland. This edition published in 2015 by NorthSouth Books.

Distributed in the United States by NorthSouth Books, Inc., New York 10016.
Library of Congress Cataloging-in-Publication Data is available.
ISBN: 978-0-7358-4210-6 (trade edition)
1 3 5 7 9 • 10 8 6 4 2
Printed in Germany by Grafisches Centrum Cuno GmbH & Co. KG, Calbe, January 2015.

www.northsouth.com

Davy
Loves the Baby

Previously published as *Will You Mind the Baby, Davy?*

Brigitte Weninger
illustrated by Eve Tharlet

Translated by Rosemary Lanning

North
South

"Children, come and hear some good news!"
called Mother Rabbit. "I'm going to have a baby."
"That's nice," said Max.
"A what?" panted Manni, rushing in.
"A baby, a new baby," murmured Lina dreamily.
"I thought I was your baby," muttered Davy.

"So," said Father Rabbit as he lit the candles,
"which do you want, a baby brother or a baby sister?"
"Either is fine with me," said Max.
"I'd like a brother," said Manni.
"No, a sister!" squealed Lina.
Davy said nothing at all.

That night Lina whispered,
"When the baby comes, there will
be seven of us—just like the seven
dwarfs. Isn't it exciting!"

Davy wasn't excited. He was wondering if he would still get second helpings of blueberries when there were seven mouths to feed. His best friend, Eddie, had a baby brother. Tomorrow he would ask him what it was like.

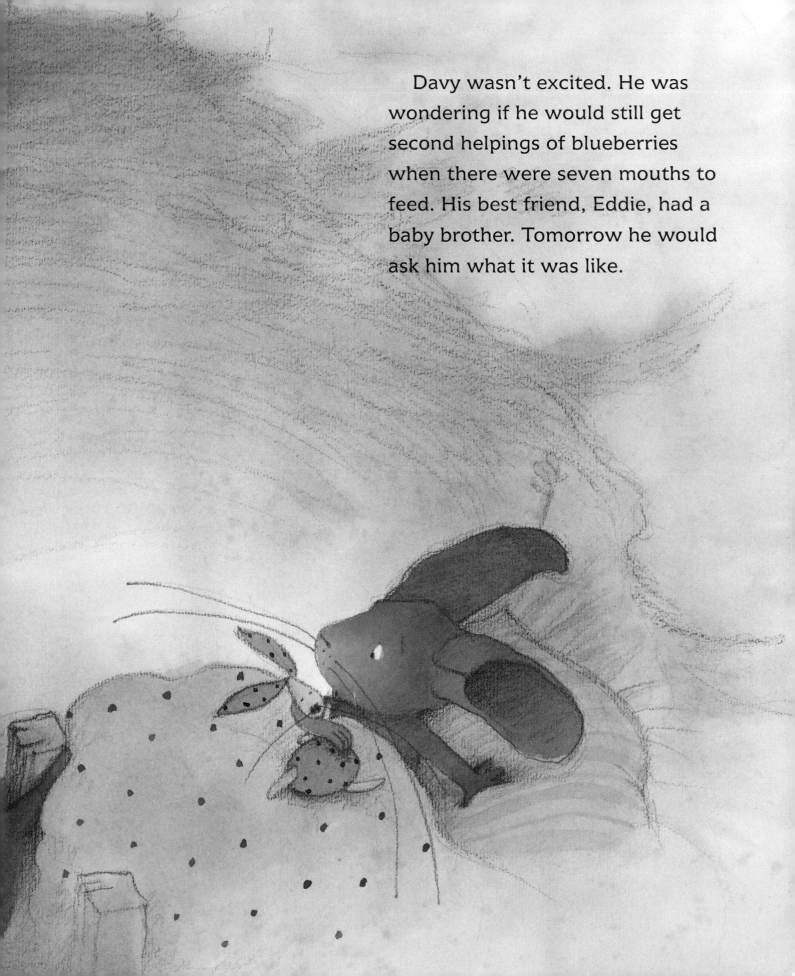

The next morning Davy found Eddie sitting in the meadow.

"Guess what," said Davy. "We're having a baby."

"Poor you," said Eddie.

"Why?" asked Davy.

Eddie thought for a moment.

Then he said, "Well, my baby brother is very small and weak, and he cries when everyone else wants to sleep. And he eats a lot. He keeps my mother busy all the time."

"Oh dear," sighed Davy. "Would a baby sister be any better?"

"Can you choose?" Eddie asked doubtfully.

"I think so," said Davy. "My father asked us which we wanted."

"Well, if you can choose, why not ask your mother for something completely different?"

"Good idea," said Davy. "Thanks, Eddie."

Davy ran to his mother. "Father asked if we wanted a baby brother or a baby sister," he said. "But I don't want either. I want a pet mouse, please."

His mother smiled. "Your father was joking," she said. "You can't really choose. The baby is already growing here." She laid Davy's paw gently on her rounded stomach. "Soon it will be born," she went on, "and then we will know if it's a baby brother or a baby sister. Try to love it either way."

"I will," said Davy quietly, but he wasn't sure he meant it.

A few days later, when the Rabbit children came back to the burrow, their mother called, "Come and meet your baby sister!"

"Aaah, isn't she beautiful," sighed Lina.

"Cute," said Max and Manni.

But Davy said, "Is she all right? She looks so floppy, and her eyes haven't opened, and she has no fur."

Mother laughed. "All baby rabbits are like that, Davy. You looked just the same." She wrapped the baby in Davy's blue blanket and passed her to Father Rabbit. "Please take the baby into the other room and let me sleep. I'm very tired."

As soon as they left the
bedroom, the baby started
to cry.

"There, there," said Father
Rabbit soothingly.

He rocked the baby gently
in his arms. But she didn't
stop crying.

"Coochee-coo," said Max, patting
the baby's bottom.

But she went on crying.

"Swing high, swing low," said Manni,
swinging the baby up and down.
   But she still cried.

"You hold her," said Lina, dumping
the baby in Davy's arms.
   "No, no, I can't," he protested.
   But the baby rested her tiny head on
Davy's shoulder and fell fast asleep.

"Well done, Davy," said Father Rabbit. Then he put his finger to his lips, and everyone tiptoed away.

All Davy could do was sit still and hold his baby sister close.

He watched her tiny whiskers tremble. Her ears were soft and downy, and almost transparent. She smelled of warm milk and fresh berries. Davy could even feel her little heart beating. He sat and gazed at her. She was so tiny. She needs someone big and strong like me to look after her, he thought.

Davy heard his mother calling for the baby.

"Here she is," he said, and he carried his little sister over to Mother's bed. "If she cries again, just call me," he said.

"Thank you, Davy," said his mother. "You are such a help to me."

Davy ran to the meadow and danced around, laughing
and singing to himself.

"What's got into you?" said Eddie.

"I have a baby sister!"

"Oh dear," said Eddie. "Does she cry a lot?"

"Not when I hold her!"

"You're kidding," said Eddie. "What do you know about
babies?"

"A lot more than you do!" said Davy, and the two of
them tumbled over the meadow, laughing and wrestling
until they were both out of breath.

Then they lay back and looked at the clouds.

Davy said, "Eddie, do you think our babies will ever be as big and strong and clever as we are?"

"Maybe, but not for a long time yet."

"You and I can look after the little ones," said Davy, "and teach them all they need to know."

"Like what?" asked Eddie.

"Like how to take extra snacks without anyone noticing, and how to look cute so Mother won't scold you if she does catch you. How to make bark boats, and whistle with grass stems . . ."

"And all the best games!" said Eddie.

"Like tag," said Davy, jumping up. "You can't catch me!"

"Oh yes, I can," said Eddie, chasing him across the meadow.